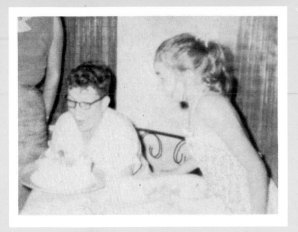

on his birthday 1951

us in 1952

Rich and me 1964

In Miami 1952

In San Francisco 1953

That night we were all out in the yard. On hot Michigan nights it was my family's custom to sleep outside, where it was cool.

"Look at those stars," Bubbie said quietly.

"Wishes are funny, aren't they," I said. "Sometimes they come true differently than you think they will."

"That's why you have to be very careful what you wish for. . . . It just may come true!" Bubbie said. Then she squeezed both of our hands. "Hang onto the grass," she whispered.

"Why, Bub?" my brother asked.

"Because if we don't, we might float up to the stars." Then she leaned over and kissed us both three times. "I kiss your eyes, and I hold both of your hearts in my good keeping. . . . And this night I thank God that I walk this earth with both of you. . . . Ah-meen!"

"You had to have stitches. . . . I watched it all!" he said excitedly.

"You fell off the merry-go-round right into some pop bottles," my gramps added.

"You even passed out!" my brother chirped. "Looks like you finally did something special!"

It was from that exact moment that our relationship changed somehow.

"Thanks, Richie," I said to him.

"What's a big brother for, anyway," he said, blushing.

The last thing I remembered was stepping off from the platform. Next thing I knew I woke up with Bubbie sitting on the edge of my bed. Mom and Grandpa were there, too.

"You gave us all a fright!" Momma said. "How do you feel?"

"What happened?" I asked.

"You fell!" my rotten redheaded older brother announced with the biggest grin on his face.

"I don't know what we would have done," my bubbie said softly. "Your brother carried you all the way home, and then he had to run to get Dr. Lee."

That night I ran straight for the merry-go-round.

We must have taken fifty turns on that carousel. But then my brother got off!

I stayed on. I went around and around and around.

"I knew I could do this longer than you," I shouted to my brother, feeling proud but just a bit dizzy.

"Treesha," I heard my bubbie call out. "Get off from that thing. . . . It's time to go home!"

The next morning all I could think about was my wish. I was thinking about it so hard I almost didn't notice the wagons and trucks pulling into the field down the road near Four Corners.

"A traveling carnival," my brother shouted as he ran toward me. "They're setting up right here in our field! Bet I can eat more hot dogs than you can," he teased.

He was already starting it, but this time I was going to do something so incredible that even he would have to sit up and take notice. I had a star wish. . . . I'd show my rotten redheaded older brother all right!"

At bedtime my bubbie came and sat on the edge of my bed like she did every night. "Look, a falling star," she said.

We watched it streak across the sky. Then she spit twice between her fingers and gave her chest a loud slap.

"Why did you do that, Bubbie?" I asked.

"I was making a wish. . . . Didn't you know that wishes on falling stars come true?"

At last I knew how I was going to get back at my brother.

For the longest time I watched the dark sky until I saw a star shoot across the night. Then I spit between my two fingers and slapped my chest.

It was done.

My wish was to do something—anything—better than my brother. I'd show him!

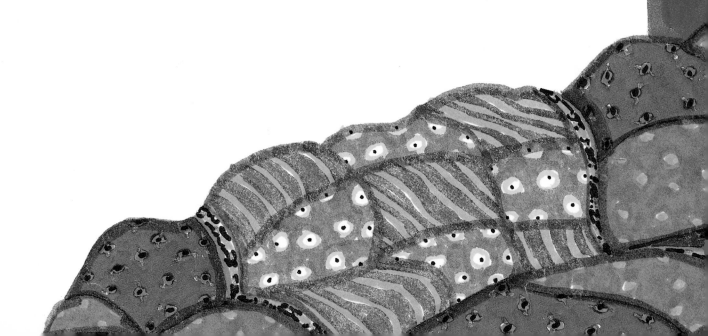

That night at dinner I could hardly eat.
"Have you been eating angry apples
again, child?" Bubbie asked as she sliced me
a huge wedge of rhubarb pie. "I baked your
favorite!"

Richard gave me one of his extra-
rotten, weasel-eyed, greeny-toothed grins.

I was so mad, I couldn't even feel how my belly was starting to ache. "I can't stand you, Richard Barber. . . . I double dog can't stand you!" I screamed as I went into the house to be consoled by my grandmother.

"Yeah, and I'm four years older than you, too, you little twerp. . . . Always have been and always will be!" he called after me. Then he laughed that rotten redheaded older brother laugh.

When I couldn't get one more sour bite into my mouth, he was still eating with relish. "I thought you said you don't like rhubarb," I said through pursed lips.

"I don't like it....I LOVE IT!" he announced as he popped the last stalk into his mouth.

Now I knew, at long last, that I had him.

"Bet I can eat more of this raw rhubarb than you can without getting the puckers!" I challenged.

"I don't think so!"

"I do!"

"I don't!" he said, narrowing his eyes.

"I do!" I insisted.

"Don't," he hissed, looking smug.

"Do," I said furiously as I grabbed the first stalk and started chewing it almost down to the leaf.

There had to be something—
SOMETHING—I could do that he couldn't!
Then an inspired thought comforted me
like a fresh breeze on a hot summer day.

"Oh, Richie," I cooed as I stood next to
the rhubarb bushes. "Do you like rhubarb?"

"No!" he said. "It's the sourest stuff on
this planet!"

get the dirtiest,

BAROOoooOOKK

burp the loudest,

and spit the farthest.

He had no equal, certainly not me!
   "And I'm four years older than you. . . .
Always have been and always will be," he
sneered.

I guess I would have to face it. He
could run the fastest,

climb the highest,

throw the farthest,

sit the longest,

"You make me sick, Richard Barber!" I yelled at him.

Then he smiled that smile that only a rotten redheaded older brother could smile.

We both picked berries for most of the afternoon.

Well, he upped and did it! He not only picked more berries than I, he set a record that wasn't even challenged for the next ten years.

"Not!" I screamed back.

There were so many things that I couldn't stand about him. The worst was that he was always telling me he could do just about everything better than I.

"Bet I can pick more blackberries than you can," he jeered at me one day.
"No you can't."
"Can so."
"Cannot!"
"Can," he whispered.
"Not," I said louder.
"Can!" he whispered so low that I could hardly hear him.

Now, I knew that she loved me all right, but I couldn't quite understand how she could even *like* my older brother, Richard. He had orange hair that was like wire; he was covered in freckles and looked like a weasel with glasses.

The one thing that my bubbie didn't seem to know was how perfectly awful my brother really was! Mind you, he was always nice whenever she was around us; but as soon as she'd leave, he would do something terrible to me and laugh.

My brother and our mother and I all lived with my grandparents on their farm in Union City, Michigan.

Now my babushka, my grandmother, knew lots of things. She knew just how to tell a good story. She knew how to make ordinary things magical. And she knew how to make the best chocolate cake in Michigan.

After she told my brother and me a grand tale from her homeland, we'd always ask, "Bubbie, is that true?"

She'd answer, "Of course is true, but it may not have happened!" Then she'd laugh.

To my brother Rich, with love
—P.P.

SIMON & SCHUSTER BOOKS FOR YOUNG READERS
An imprint of Simon & Schuster Children's Publishing Division
1230 Avenue of the Americas
New York, New York 10020
Copyright © 1994 by Patricia Polacco
All rights reserved including the right of reproduction in whole or
in part in any form.
Simon & Schuster Books for Young Readers
is a trademark of Simon & Schuster.
This book is set in Cochin.
The illustrations were done in marking pens and pencil.
Manufactured in the United States of America
10 9 8 7 6 5 4 3 2
Library of Congress Cataloging-in-Publication Data
Polacco, Patricia.
  My rotten redheaded older brother / by Patricia Polacco.
    p. cm.
  Summary: After losing running, climbing, throwing, and burping
competitions to her obnoxious older brother, a young girl makes a wish
on a falling star.
  [1. Brothers—Fiction. 2. Sibling rivalry—Fiction.] I. Title.
PZ7.P75186My 1994 [E]—dc20 93-13980 CIP AC
ISBN: 0-671-72751-6

Richie and me 1951

on the farm 1948

Richie and me 1954

on the farm 1948